DESTINY OF A
HOMIE WARRIOR

JOSEPH TUCKER

Printed in the United States of American

First printing, 2021

ISBN: 978-0-578-98467-4

Email: stacie_tucker@charter.net

A Mother's Love

--- ★ ⭐ ★ ---

I can't tell you how proud I am of my son for finishing his first book as a self published Author. You see, it's extra special because he was diagnosed with Autism at the age of 3. He couldn't talk. I was told by doctors that he would have this label forever and basically to just give up on him. Of course, I didn't. I sought out on a journey and path to get help not only for Autism resources, but also searching for that needle... that needle in a haystack to find his knitch. I found it! With God's help; it was in writing. He loved to read and eventually wanted to write. The library was a candy store for him from pretty much a year old. He finally started talking at age 5, things took off from there and the rest is history. He received nothing short of a Miracle!

I love you~ Mom

Dedications:

To my mom, Stacie Tucker for not just giving up on me but being there for me. And to my dad, Jimmy Tucker for providing the financial resources.

Acknowledgement:

First, I want to give thanks to God. I want to thank my manager Aunt Pam, my Dad, Close Friends and Family in general. And most importantly to you guys, my supporters.

BASED ON A TRUE STORY

Contents

— ★ ★ ★ —

Chapter 1

Alter Egos

— ★ ⭐ ★ —

Introduction

I spiritually believe in a curse. It's sometimes like a spell that says pure evil by something or someone going by how it is, or who they are, either way cursed in general. Everyone has a destiny including my own but I think the reason why is because of what we went through causing evil to strike from person to person. That someone who wears t-shirts with no open toe shoes that are sneakers, rocks a fro and someone with caramel skin along with a HomieWarrior necklace with my initials on it, and is sometimes seen as different from others. Believe it or not, that's me. My name is Joseph, but everyone calls me Joe.T. I named myself that.

Olde savannah, a suburban place where I said my first word (cuss word), a place that didn't just look nice but how we stand up for what we believe in, and how everybody who had a place in my heart lived there, but also in my hometown of the state Georgia in the Suwanee~ Atlanta area, and some in Memphis, Tennessee where my mom lived. My school is in Gwinnett County and is kinda d fferent from my home life. So when I'm there, I'm still me. Basically, Joe.T is not just a nickname but more of an alter ego. The same with Joseph, my real name of course.

Everybody has something unique to their persona which mine pretty much says: chilled, creative, sarcastic, down to earth, can be savage, dope, real and just all of the above. But besides that, I guess the term Homiewarrior is like you're a real ride or die with the people you mess with and how as if you're a warrior who you fight your battles with, but it's the metaphor for me. Anyways, I never knew that bad can turn into worse. I never knew that trouble can lead to a destiny along with friends and family being into it. So much drama that was going on from time to time it all felt like another lifetime movie but in reality, of evil as it was spiritually or at least felt like it, but still part of the curse.

Sometimes you just don't want any drama but people will still hurt you even if you're unbothered, doing your own thing or they don't know what you go through as you wonder why. Whether it's a struggle that not everybody experiences except when there were regular days as usual, but the unusual when you never know if it happens.

Chapter 2

Facts & Receipts
Of The Lifestyle

─────────── ⋆ ★ ⋆ ───────────

But let's start all the way back from the beginning. Back when I was just one of the any other type of people you would know, a regular nobody. Okay, not really a nobody but really just happily an average person with savage moments here and there but still somewhat regular. Anyways. I was diagnosed with autism when I was like 3 years of age as I obviously didn't understand. So of course, I barely remember. Even though I am kind of seen as different, I don't mention it too much because I honestly just act and see myself as regular but with character. So, after going from program to program for you know, my mild disorder, not talking much when I was little and blah blah blah. I was still n special ed but it wasn't like going from mental hospital to mental hospital where for me it was confusing and just complicated.

Glenwood, where I've been many times. Especially when we went to church. It's always the same usual routine. Get ready for church, go to church in a hood area which is Glenwood that's next to the barbershop and besides the other church that used to sell bread and sometimes has a barbeque where the fence is. Going through traffic we make it to whether we're almost early or late when the service is almost over. But it's whatever, anyway me and mom (Stacy) who is the first lady walk in and sit by my sister, Niya. Well, she's not my sister- sister she's my God sister even though we're not related or blood to blood I still consider her my sister. After the choir sings my dad (Jim) who's the pastor goes up and obviously preaches for half an hour and I collect the offering towards the end of service. I go up to get the basket and Dad says our prayer as everybody puts money in the basket along with everybody puts money in the basket along with everyone conversing. Plus, I go to the office, leave the basket and let sister Felicia handle the cash tithes and offering.

Then there's the gas station or corner store that me and Niya go out to get some snacks from time to time as we walk. And once when those lights go out, church comes to a close as we leave from the dark.

Scooter as they called me, they still do, but not as much anymore since around junior high was when I legally changed my nickname to my real name, Joseph. As we were walking out the church, me and Niya just talked about life as we conversed a lot every single Sunday which was the only time we were able to see each other in person. Then here comes Niya's sister from her birth mom, Keyshaya with her little kids, Deshawn, Payton and Sephen. They are not really family members of mine, just people I knew. Alright y'all c'mon she says to her children, she is crazy, Niya says as I crack up laughing. I get in the car, me and Niya say bye as mom drives off. Looking out the window I see the church that's across our church. The other church is where you go to get splashed, well baptized, have long hours of service, and can be a little too religious. We went before but now we don't go there.

Anyways, Elementary school was just early childhood, nothing much. Before puberty, hormones and realizing your growing up. It was okay, activities that I never cared for. I transferred from another school district because of some rude teacher who I forgot about. I never thought about transferring but mom did, so I just acted as if I got expelled from that school.

I usually watched my all-time favorite, "That's so raven." I still do now, but for reruns. Great sitcoms, but only if it had a better ending. From time to time, I went to see my best friend Sith the ongest. I went over to his house, we both said hey and never got bored but entertained each other when just talking and conversing about random stuff even when he had a party at his house. He can be somewhat in his world, but he's cool as we go to the mall or hangout.

Overall, my backup plan was to be a rapper and other opportunities, even somebody at the church recommended I should be signed to a record label and put in work in the studio. Like producing beats, music, a way to express lyrically, imagery (Music videos) and performally, if that's even a word. Dad finding out I freestyle is why he constantly preaches about celebrities or their scandals. I think he preached just to turn his life around but hey that's just me. Besides that, I did Youtube videos and other social media, trying to promote merchandise and other side hustles that come with shenanigans and antics that could be resolved. Music was plan B or like another outlet. A career that wasn't an evolved career. Yet anyway I get being a diva, selling yourself out, and having 15 minutes of fame, then being well known along with being in the right path rather than the wrong path. Being obsessive, preaching about this subject even from junior high is a bit too much.

When it came to style, I wore what fits me like it's my own merchandise. Going through a phase happens if it's something ridiculous, but I just wanted to have an image of being me because I didn't want to lose myself and not be a poser for anyone else when beauty is in the inside and what you think is confident within your style. As corny and cheesy it may sound, your soul and persona is how you come off to be is the definition of your character, even if somebody pissed you off to make you out of character that is enough of my somewhat pep talk.

And lastly Dofflotwo.net which is just random or relatable segments that's a creation that was just come up with even from Sith and Aundru which the segments remind of random topics me and Sith just talked about as it is used as an idea sometimes for a side hustle which again is a walk of life.

But this event is more than just a main plot of a lifestyle. More than relatable scenarios like an episode. Before school came around summer break was on the rise. Yeah, it was cool, but later on it became more unexpected. Whether it was vacations interrupted, mental health or just being toxic and messy. It all goes not just downhill, but gets way deeper from here.

Chapter 3

Trauma But I Got Over It

— ★ ★ ★ —

Earlier before school.

It was just like any other day. Months after freshman year me and Mom were on vacation. Niya usually goes with us, but this time she didn't as I wish she would've, especially at this exact moment. We were staying at a hotel room as it just wasn't all that great. Anyway, same with the pool and the service of breakfast. As we went to bed that night that's when fate started to hit. Once again, I hear my ringtone as I wake up. My phone is out of control. And of course, I see who it is, and unexpectedly Dad is calling. I answered. Why? Because I was already wondering why is someone calling me this early at like 5,6 or 7 am in the morning, and plus I was already annoyed. He tells me why he didn't call Mom's phone as I wondered, but I was obviously too worn out to think about it. Mom is wide awake as I give her my phone. And her being cranky as well, I hand her the phone as she answers when wearing her head scarf like she does every night. WHAT! she yelled! She jumps out of the restroom to go talk privately. At first before the call, I thought it was just a typical wrong number phone call that everyone goes through. I didn't want to pick it up, but

I picked up. Anyways, I lay down on my silk pillowcase and try to go back to sleep. But I couldn't, and then that's when the trouble of suspense came out. Dad breaks the news that Grandma (Ria) is here in my hometown,Suwanee, Atlanta Georgia. She snuck on the bus, paid her ticket, and traveled all the way from Memphis, Tennessee to downtown Atlanta at the bus stop without Mom's permission or not even letting us know that she was coming. She just showed up when we're far away from home. Dad picks her up instead of taking her home like my mom suggested. Mom calls Grandma to confront her as Grandma yells, cusses Mom out, and I realize that my grandma is not in the right state of mind. And me, I'm just silent with no words. We cancel the trip, pack up our stuff, leave the hotel, get in the car and rush home. We only stayed there for one day but didn't care for it. Anyways, DAMN! Can't even have a vacation without something happening! Mom rants. And to make things worse the car started to have a problem as I heard Mom crying but tried to stay strong as the car faithfully kept going on the highway during traffic.

We make it home as we wonder where she can be all around the city of Atlanta. It turns out she's at sister Felicia's house(a sister who I don't even consider a Nun). Dad dropped her off there basically instead of attempting to try to get her back on the bus as they said a prayer for her from what I heard. We head over there and at the porch we see sister Felicia and Raj, her son, as we converse. That's when we see Grandma as she gets in the passenger seat. Her hair wasn't even brushed, her baggy eyes looked possessed, and the way she was dressed just shows that all she did was come out of the house. We headed off to traffic and Mom asked, Mama, why did you come here when we were gone? Mom asks angrily. Grandma just vents constantly. Then we get home. The last thing I knew was how she recognized how much I've grown and her venting about getting hit by her husband but enough wasn't enough.

The next morning everything seemed just normal. Aunt Jemima pancakes along with of course syrup and butter that Mom cooked, us watching tv on a Saturday morning and Grandma waking up as usual. It was fine but unfortunately it didn't last long. It wasn't until she started making a disturbance as Mom had to leave the office at our house where she works. You need to go to the doctor, she says which triggers Grandma. I ain't going nowhere Stacy, grandma shouts! Oh, you're getting outta here to get some help, mom said! You going, she yelled! She goes off as I hear Mom and Grandma yelling and screaming downstairs in the kitchen. I leave my room as I grab my suitcase and spazz out. I called Niya by accident and let Mom hang up the phone as I left for Grandma. I mention and call out all the stuff from yesterday. Not even as revenge but just out of anger. I meant to grab her suitcase, but I was too angry that I got the wrong one. I told her I'm running away and by running away I mean running from her drama. As I constantly tell her to go, leave and just snap. Threats being thrown and said, and out and pretty much it was just family drama that everyone goes through in their household, but no sign of peace whatsoever. I ran upstairs, still going off at Grandma. GO HOME! I repeat. I go into Mom's room and I stand at the window. Grandma tried to explain herself but I was not for it. I'm leaving you. Just stop! You upset me! Mom! Just everybody in this family! I yelled. Mom tries to calm me down by holding me. Move, I repeated. But of course she didn't let go as I started breaking down. One droplet of a tear that came out of my eye was all I could take as I breathed hard aggressively. Grandma tries to talk to me. JUST SHUT UP! I start throwing pillows at her. Get Out Of Here! Get Out, I snapped! She walks away. After Mom calmed me down, I went to my room as the suspense moved again. Mama! you need to stop! You are even making Joseph upset, Mom confronts. I DON'T CARE! She screams. You want me to call lakeside, mom threatens. It sets Grandma off even more when she starts breaking down, cries, and gets even more aggressive. GO TO HELL! FORGET ALL YALL! she snaps. Okay, that's it, I'm calling, mom says. She gets 911 on the phone line. Sooner or later cop cars and medical facilities start swarming across the neighborhood and people start looking out their windows. I step out of my room, hide behind the wall, and watch the whole scene unfold. Grandma starts going off at the authorities and Mom just sobs because she had to call the police on her own mom. And what really sets her off is that Mom and the authorities address her mental illness with Schizophrenia. Mom explains the symptoms, but doesn't go into details since most of it is kind of personal or at least how Grandma took it. Minutes later Grandma is being escorted, taken away, and sent to a lakeside mental hospital. I just watched, feeling concerned as I felt like when I closed my memory constantly as everything faded to black.

My memory looks up. We're at the hospital because Mom needed to drop off Grandma's stuff since she forgot and left it in the guest room. I'm sitting in the lobby waiting. Me and Mom leave the Lakeside Hospital as I sense she's here, there, anywhere. I even had dreams of the incident that same night that I felt the suspense and drama. Just fate in general, I can feel it, I felt it. Mom calls me down for breakfast. I can barely eat, feeling like I'm about to throw up. Dad talked with me about it, but it didn't help. He just wanted to put his two cents in by rubbing it in so I barely even listened. It's Grandma, she wants to talk to you, Mom says. I got the phone. Grandma starts to apologize about what happened yesterday. I forgive you, but Grandma you need help, I answer as she obviously agreed. I was guessing she apologized because she thought that Mom and I mostly were about to hold a grudge. Hours later, we visited Grandma at the lakeside Hospital. She was looking rough and not well, especially when the doctors kept giving her medication that still didn't help her disorder let alone the way of how they kept treating her. After minutes of conversing, visiting hours are over. We say goodbye and me and Mom leave. We get in the car and head home. I'm going to drop off your grandma at the bus station. Are you coming, Mom asked? I said no, but hoped Grandma would make it on the bus. So mom left.

I got over this incident a week later because I ended up getting used to it just like how I've been getting use to what runs through the family for years, which is dysfunction and mental health. Mom kept hiding it about grandma because she didn't want me to know, but I already knew. The pills, what she sees, the voices inside her head, the medicine she takes every day in a week, and the outbursts she has from time to time like when she went off on uncle Sails when I was little. But I was way too young to understand, so it was like what more can I do. But from the day during that summer when I saw that side of her, it's like I didn't even know who she was anymore. I thought it was just a mental breakdown, but still had that same soul the whole family was used to seeing. I didn't think it would get this bad to the point where she was off her meds. Except for her meds, she stopped taking them for a whole month or longer.

Mom comes back from a stressful moment of taking Grandma to the bus stop so she can go home as she takes a break from work. I could pretend that nothing happened,but I would be blunt about this since I've been blunt about my home life which is not any different, but still crazy. Even Mom wished this never happened ,and she's right this was not supposed to happen, but it did. It was unexpected which is why one person including me is either crushed, feels dead inside, traumatized, disappointed, but not surprised. And grandma, one who has to be sent back to their hometown, Memphis, to go to a mental hospital or as I call it, to go to prison for people with mental health issues.

As it's being heard, just in case, nobody wins in this. Everything with that incident was like a psych ward tragedy, a terror of making a scene in public and in front of company or one moment of rage or professional help she never got as she's considered "just crazy" as people thought. That incident was complete bs. It isn't just something that is relatable that happens all the time on a daily basis or just happens overnight. This is a kind of incident where there's a reason when this drove her on the edge for me and Mom to see our own mother and grandmother be mentally ill. The reason is family dysfunction that I and some are used to seeing, but slowly was burning and becoming a game of fire with the fire and then it, KABOOM! This incident probably was going on for a long while in Grandma's household even before vacation, and even if I moved on there's still unanswered questions of the reason for why she did this in the first place.

Chapter 4

My Somewhat
Best Of Dark Guilt

— ★ ★ ★ —

S ummer break ends as school comes around. Everybody starts talking about how their summer went, and what classes they're taking. The first day was the pep rally with takes place in the gym. So me and Sith go sit on the bleachers. Cheerleaders, mascots and loud music playing in the background. I kept my fingers crossed hoping nobody would ask me about my summer, but to be honest with myself, realistic and having logic of course, I knew they would ask what happened on my summer break. Like I said before, I got over the incident with my grandma originally a week later. Because I knew that not only, I didn't like holding grudges when it comes to people who screw up unintentionally, but I knew that I couldn't be traumatized in a furious angered way forever. I knew I had to continue to live my life. Usually, I moved on and tried to enjoy the pep ra ly, but still kept quiet a little bit.

Days later I'm walking on the track, fitness walk. Sith comes to me, I keep walking. He made it to my direction as he followed. He asked me the same question just like everyone else asked. Are you okay? I say, yes, I'm fine. Why does everyone keep asking that, I said in frustration. Because you're acting weird, you've been so quiet lately. What's going on dude, he asks? This basically ends up turning into a you know me; I know you more than anyone type of discussion.... Eh, just some issues in my home life, it's nothing, forget it. But either way I'm fine. I'm just tired, I explain. Okay then, Sith says. After the dark guilt that was eating me alive was out of the way, we both walked together at the fitness walk and just conversed about life and random stuff as usual like we always do. It's hard, but I know that life is short. I had to choose to move on.

Chapter 5

Life Of The Party
Besides Fake Friends

— ⋆ ★ ⋆ —

Seeing the people you've known for years face to face once again, and some you will never see again after a semester. I've had my moments with close friends and family (Junior High Middle School and High School at times mainly). But, I just consider it to be moments to take place in a somewhat school setting because it just didn't take place there. Because it was also home and other places. I don't just have my Bff and closest friend Sith, but other c ose friends who are with me as we walk through the crowded hallways looking fresh and fly since there's people around. Just kidding. We just walk and act natural because we just don't care. Especially i⁻ it's in front of the whole world. Some of them just talk, some of them just make out in the corner, anc some of them are on the phone and just stare. They stared as I rolled my eyes. And that was the sign of me not giving two birds and bees. Really glowed up some guys with they're sixpacks while I glowed but still looked the same. No six pack, husky body with skinny stomach but flab on my thighs. Anyways, Nio goes and chats with his other group of friends and how the social is genuine and not fake or pretend. And Aundru.......well, me, Sith, Nio and everyone else who knew him for a long time were still close friends with him, but not everybody hangs out with him too much. Especially when he had problems with his temper, but he could control himself. Kind of a geeky type of friend at that, but still cool. It's somewhere in my own little world where if I mark you off the list and you're done and cut off. I still believe in forgiveness and giving chances unless you keep betraying my trust by constantly being messed up by doing toxic stuff. But for the most part I can just be neutral when it comes to my friendliest and by friendliest, I mean a real friendship with also family that are people I actually care about.

And oh, as we walk down the hallway, I see a familiar face. It was him, Camryn. Oh yeah, that was the guy who was my neighbor that moved away and whom I got into a fight with. Followed by him trying to ruin my image with "rumors". But it obviously failed, as me and my friends brought up a flashback later on. We basically are kind of cool with him, but like I said I can be neutral, as in this case it's what I am when it comes to this guy. Me and my close friends basically just consider him the insecure one out of everybody in the whole world. He is the type of person that would talk stuff about someone, but has higher levels of insecurities that shows about himself and tries to have confidence.

Whatever. All I know is that I wasn't in the mood or was sick of the drama from my home life and at school, heck maybe even with all the fake friends and beefs. I just wanted to find peace since I was fed up. Not saying it was always toxic but here and there. Just like vacation before trouble came. Everyone else went to six flags, waterparks, etc. I had to witness a mental breakdown from a family member.

Nio and I are cool. I see Rem with his emo haircut, color dye hair, and dark wardrobe giving gothic vibes. It looked cool, but we were just associates that said hi and bye. Me and Josh are considered mutual friends. And I don't know what's been up with me and Jamie lately. Just an analogy but me and my close friends are like cheetah girls, but male versions. We've known each other with a friendship forever. Speaking of forever. Before I met Aundru and Nio. Sith and I have known each other for the longest time since we were little, as closest best friends as I hope it stays that way. Always.

I am just trying to enjoy the life of the party by trying to protect my peace for now and try to think of what I went through as no big deal which feels normal for me. I do be blunt about home life, but at the same time I don't mention it too much because I don't want anyone to feel bad for me. And sometimes I might hate it when I do that but I do it so it won't be used as an excuse anyway.

Chapter 6

Sexuality

★ ★ ★

Flashback to June.

Found out I'm an asexual. Or ace for short. I knew I was, but didn't know much of the word just yet. I told Niya first. She was the first person I ever came out too. She accepted it a little. Then I told close friends Sith,Nio and Aundru. They accepted, but just didn't really care. Almost everybody knew about my sexuality except for Mom and Dad. At first, I wondered what if I told my parents, what would they say or think about me. I still haven't told them yet. But it didn't matter. Even if I typically get disowned or kicked out of the house, that's fine. I would rather they know that I told them. So whatever happens, then just let it be whether they accept that I barely have no sexual attraction or not.

Chapter 7

Death /The Funeral

$\star$ ★ $\star$

It was the day that my grandma from my dad's side of the family passed away. We always called her Big Momma even though she wasn't big we still nicknamed her that anyway. In a flashback we pull up at the funeral and park where the parking lot was as we get through traffic. The funeral was so crowded that it was so hard to find a parking spot, but we parked somewhere eventually. We finally get inside the funeral home. I walked in, and there she was lying peacefully in the casket. She was still wearing her church hat along with the dress and heels. I can feel her spirit leaving this earth as my hand accidentally almost touches her casket where there is the corpse, but I try to stay still as I take one final look to watch her one last time. Me, Mom and Dad walked to one of the benches and sat. Some people had tissues with tear prints on it of course and the entire time the pastor talks about her memories before she died. Some I do kind of remember. The time that Mom always had to drop Big Momma off to her retirement home after church, Dad's stories he used to tell when preaching about his mom, and also when she embarrassed us at a fancy restaurant we went to. We did not know that she was going through Alzheimer's. I bet her soul thinks about her son every single day.

The funeral is over hours later. We leave the car as I see people struggling to carry the casket along with her body to the grave at the decomposed graveyard where flowers are placed at the tombstones. We head to the car and leave the funeral home as I see my Dad tearing up obviously because of the loss of his mother. Sweetie, are you crying, Mom asked as she calls him, they're "romantic" names like they usually do . Nah sweetie, I just got something in my eyes dad said, it's just watery or something, you know I got cataracts and stuff he denies. Mom knows he's lying, but she doesn't say anything because of how hurt he was. It was the first time I ever saw tears from him. Of course, I felt bad even if we never had a father-son relationship yet which I might explain later on. But her in heaven is more than daddy issues, as I leave it to the side.

As I remember going to supreme fish, the restaurant that was close to the church that Big Momma liked going to, or Dad's funny comedic stories that involved his mom. And there it goes. The supreme fish restaurant was shut down for good that was close to church and got replaced with a burger place. It was like, well dang, once she left the planet along with her spirit it's like she took everything she loved, adored and what she will always remember with her from the world ever since she was pronounced dead and gone to heaven. She may be resting in peace, but she's not gone. When people die, they don't just disappear in thin air. She's gone but not forgotten. She's good in a better place.

Chapter 8

Daddy Issues +
Almost Got Evicted

★ ★ ★

Me and Dad never really had a father-son relationship. But it wasn't like he just left my mom when she was pregnant with me just like how a dirty dog would. But he just came and went as he would always be at work and by work I mean just be gone all the time. He would usually come home around Sundays, but it would either be late at night or around dinner. I get the questions. Where's your dad? Was your dad ever there for you? How come I never see your dad? And sometimes I wondered the same thing. Even close friends, especially when I was younger would ask. But I ended up getting used to my dad being gone all the time when I got older. Despite the toxic arguments we and Mom and Dad had, him not going on vacation, and constantly getting married and divorced three times with child support and a drug dealing criminal record past behind his back, I will say this. He did help out with the mortgage/rent to keep a roof over our head except for when he made this big mistake. It was the day we went to court because Dad trusted this lady at his job when he had the store at the time or just businesses which he still has like the restaurant, convenience stores and obviously the church. Even though that man has diabetes, he still woke up walking with a limp, hurting while going from Georgia to Alabama where most of his businesses were located.

When we were in the courtroom it wasn't just court day it was an eviction notice where we were almost about to lose the house because of the woman Dad trusted which obviously he had to fight back in court/ trial. The last thing I remember was that dad planned to sue. The results were that we were able to keep the house, which is a blessing, when we left the courtroom. He was there for me, when it came to a roof over our head, yes but no when it came to spending time with me or with family. I still love my dad, because family is family no matter what, but I still would admit that we had a love-hate relationship. So many people say that I am just like my dad,which is the reason why we don't talk that much as things would get better or worse in my home life, but it didn't phase me. It just felt like that was just a part of me.

Chapter 9

Church In The Ghetto

★ ★ ★

After service the church next door or the purple church as we call it where the fence is, was having a barbeque/cookout. I got my plate and filled it up with burgers and hot dogs as I had to cover my plate from flies since we were eating outside. After dessert and everyone talking for hours, Mom was finally ready to leave after me, waiting for her since she would always talk for hours when there's company around. She says goodbye as we get in the car and leave. Mom starts to talk about quitting the choir. She usually sings in the choir group but not anymore. I guess her choir group days are over. Or mainly because of some of the members being loco or coming from jealousy and being fake as things just end up ugly. It was just...toxic, Mom says in confession. Toxic? I repeat. Yes, Toxic Mom confesses again. I think it's about everybody I say. What do you mean, she asked? The people in society, some people in church, mainly choir groups and toxic energy and all of the above, I explained. Yep, that's why I quit the choir because it's just a bunch of haters that want to be toxic and messy. Just mostly females always gotta be hating. That's why I barely have female friends, Mom says. Males can be messy too, I agreed. But they're not as feisty like some of us females Mom corrects.

Also, I barely think about school and how I'm not too focused as Mom mentions. You're barely focusing. I'm barely focused on anything because I don't care about the basic population of history, dividing math problems, or stuff that I don't need for the future. The only thing I care about and is contemplating, the only thing that still hurts, and the only thing that is stuck on my mind mostly is why did that incident with Grandma happened or occurred and the toxic warzone or battle in the church along with this curse. And how I want to hurt a nemesis that is just like them as much as they hurt close friends and family,but most of all as much as they hurt me.

Chapter 10

A Regretful Wedding

— ★ ★ ★ —

Niya can be a little overprotective and too loyal. She's cool. Even though she begged us to let her stay at our house because she didn't want to go home, she had no choice and cried. Her husband or as I still consider a boyfriend who's a douchebag, Terry lives there. How was he a husband? She didn't want to marry him, but her birth mom forced her to.

Flashing to her wedding. Everybody was dressed formally of course. I didn't mind dressing formally, but I hated wearing those fancy suits. It may have been way too fancy but of course I did it for not just the occasion but for Niya. I see her walk as the bride with the white dress. She's smiling, but I can tell she didn't want to do this. The whole marriage was so forced. It looked like nobody wanted to be in there, especially me and Mom because we knew Niya's birth mom forced her to do this. Dad, being the reverend, marries Niya and Terry together as husband and wife. Then there's the speak now or forever hold your peace saying. Everybody was just silent. Mom wanted to say something, but she just kept quiet. I knew this would have ruined the moment, so I just shut up too and waited for this to be over. As I move on from this predictable cliché's moment where Niya and Terry kiss when Dad says you may kiss the bride after he asks them do you take her/him to be husband/wife as they say I do forcefully. Everyone congratulates them and after we have the wedding cake Niya regrets getting married because he seemed non-trustworthy and also because of Niya's history of having cheating boyfriends. Even if Niya didn't wanna go home I can see why she didn't want to.

Her sister Keyshaya always has Niya babysit her kids while she goes out having fun. Basically, have Niya take care of her Baby daddy Drama and neglected responsibility. And also, how her Birth mom, and the people around her in her household took advantage of her. Even if she had to go home, I still felt bad and saw the reason why she wanted to stay with us.

Anyway, around the morning me and Mom talk as she mentions Camryn like she did before. Mom, you never liked him, well at least not as much I say. She starts mocking him by moving her body side to side while stomping on her feet as I snicker. Even when me and Camryn were somewhat friends and when he did the same position Mom did because he missed the bus and asked Mom for a ride to school. I will admit it was downright low, but Mom being funny I couldn't help but to let out a little laugh.

Chapter 11

The Fight!

— ★ ★ ★ —

Speaking of Camryn: basically, the flashback fight. The sad thing about this was we used to be friends. But that's when it all changed. Location:Cafeteria | We need to talk. I say, about what, Camryn asks? I address the issues we had but then he talks about his issues. What really irked me about Camryn is that I remember when I said Camryn is seen as the most insecure one out of everybody in the world. Well, this shows. Of course, he has problems just like everyone else, but it's like at this moment from what irked me when he used it as an excuse. Really! I snapped as I rolled my eyes. So, I guess we're not gonna be friends, he says. I give him the stink eye as I cross my arms. At this point I guess not, I say. This whole thing didn't feel like an argument, it was just disgusting looks, and just saying stuff back and forth to each other. Joseph, why can't you just get over it, he asks? I already have, but you know what, maybe Nio was right about you, I said. About what, he snapped! That you are a fake I insult. He moves his body towards me like he's about to do something as I do the same. We stomp away as I chuck the deuces at him.

Destiny of a Homie Warrior

The next day, I talked to Nio about it. Even he suspected Camryn was a fake. I always knew sometimes me and Camryn had our shady moments, but I was still kinda cool with him because of his attitude and his positive personality from time to time. So I was still cool with him up until now. Next thing you know Camryn shows up and walks to our table. Crap, Camryn, I muttered. He probably overheard me and thought I was talking crap. Camryn comes over and gives me a cookie like that is gonna bribe me to be friends with him again. You wouldn't, I doubt. Okay what do you want, seriously Nio says. Camryn just scoffs. Leave him out of this, I say. I put the cookie aside. Thank you, but just cut the crap already. I know the only reason you came over here is just because you overheard me talking about you, I point out. Fine, I understand, he says in manipulation. BOOM! He trips and falls on one of the seats and falls on the ground. Ha, I say! He swings at me with his gray hoodie. I dodge it. No! Joseph No! He snapped and walked away in a rage and has a death stare like a whole new level of "enemies". I took a bite and spit out the cookie because I thought it was poison.

Friday comes around as our "beef" becomes a whole new level. I was about to dump chocolate milk in the trash. I forgot about the "beef" since I thought it wasn't worth it and thought he's just weird with insecurities being his weakness. I felt a shove and it was Camryn. I noticed because of his gray hoodie. I sneaked and ran to him with the chocolate milk still in my hand. He swats it. Chocolate milk gets all over the cafeteria floor. I almost slipped. I kicked it back to him. The milk gets on his shoes. That's it! This time you went too far so I snapped. I rolled my sleeves as I balled my fist up. Camryn steps out of the lunch line and puts his tray to the side. What, you wanna go, he says! We stared like we wanted to kill each other. We push, punches being swung, hands being thrown along with slaps to the face. It starts to gather a crowd. Obviously, everyone watches. I yell in rage. I grabbed him by his hood and the back of his hoodie and swung him across the cafeteria with a kick and a hit acting like I jumped him. He lands, bumps and falls on the tables. Again, it wasn't karma this time. No one jumped in to try to break it up. It was me with my pissed off emotions and the strength of don't mess with me. Administrators or security guards get involved, cuss words, N words etc. fly out my mouth as I run to grab my lunch and sit next to Nio. I can tell he was shocked by seeing the whole thing unfold as me and Camryn are both called into the office, separately of course. We both get sentenced to ISS (In School Suspension). I go back to the lunch room. Woah, what happened, Nio asked? I don't want to talk about it, I say. I didn't go into details knowing that everybody saw it. Duh!

I got home knowing they called my mom, but I was prepared to get yelled at. Boy, what happened at school today, mom confronted me. Me and Camryn got into a fight simply as that, I explained. I knew this was gonna happen, she predicted.

After ISS the whole school was still talking about it and exaggerating it. People in the crowd either laughed, chanted ooh! or wanted to know what happened. Probably a combination of all three. I've been through fights physically and verbally or both, but I never considered myself a fighter because I never started nor tried to pick fights or attack people for no reason. Some people just wanted to try me. Basically, I never picked, chose or started my battles. My battles started, and I got picked because they chose me.

Chapter 12

"Rumors"

— ★ ★ ★ —

The fight wasn't even enough to let go or squash this "beef". A semester later rumors started going around. It was spreading like when you whisper a rumor in someone's ear. The energy is contagious. Especially when they say pass it on. I walked down the hallway minding my own business. I wondered about the fight Camryn and I had from last semester. I'm sure people had gotten over it by now, but who knows, people probably had their phones out. I might've ended up on world star a.k.a one of the most ratchet websites. No one recorded though like they usually do, but if they did, I wouldn't be surprised if I saw myself being aggressive on the internet. Even during the fight, he was trying to man up like what guys usually do.

Following after I fought him, I yelled, I CAN'T BELIEVE I WAS EVER FRIENDS WITH YOU, I shouted! Minutes later I get sent to the principal's office. Usually, the school will call you on the intercom which they still do or they just give you a pink slip. I go to the office, I'm not worried because I didn't do anything but just was confused. I go to the lobby and sit on the bench. They call me in and I sit in front of the desk. There's like 3 or 4 administrators. They start asking questions that I wasn't aware of then. That's when they give me some information on why they brought me here. Long story short, some student told the administrator that I assaulted Camryn. Wait a minute! Hold up (pause)! What in the actual hell? I look like what is wrong with you? And all I can do is just say what?! But I thought about it, and knew what was going on here. Camryn started the rumor just to get back at me from our fight in the cafeteria, but I didn't mention it to the principal or administrators. All I did was prove, explain myself and told them that somebody was lying on me and had my name in their mouth when it came to any type of assault, battery, or whatever it was. You can go back to class now, they finally said. I knew in my heart and soul it was Camryn who started these stupid rumors, but I didn't want to jump into conclusions too quick as I left out of the office suspiciously.

A day later, I walked down the hallway hearing whispers. I hear Jamie talking about the so-called incident with my name in his mouth. I confronted him. What are you guys talking about? Of course, they typically say, uh nothing. It's about me and Camryn isn't it, I say as I cross my arms. Jamie just heard about it as the guy who he's talking to tells me to go to class. Alright, I'll go, but this isn't over I say as a warning. I continue walking as everybody looks at me while talking and whispering. I tell myself to run like a mob is after me but I fast walk. Pushed with confrontations, lies being thrown, and this rumor being talked about as a conversation is like actual school news that is part of the announcements.

The next day, I saw Sith and Aundru. At first, I thought they were talking about the rumors as I almost said... you too, but it was some other stuff. Camryn stalked them at lunch. What the hell? First, dumb rumors about me going around, now he's stalking you guys at lunch, I said. I find it funny when he does this when I'm not around. I talked with Jamie. I just heard about it, he says again. So even if you were just talking about it with someone the other day you didn't start the rumor. So, if it wasn't you then who was it- CAMRYN! I knew it, I said! Trying to turn people against me with false assumptions. I wish he could just go away. I know, Sith says. I just got there that morning and now I'm having a reputation. I knew he was trying to get me back because of the fight we had last semester in the cafeteria. Wait, you guys got into a fight, Aundru asks? I told Sith what happened but not Aundru. Yes, and now he has spread this failed rumor around not just because he doesn't like me now, but because of him trying to get revenge on me for the fight I'm telling you guys about, I explained. It's true, Sith says. At least you guys believe me, I said. We do, especially since you believe Camryn was stalking us at lunch Aundru says. I tell Aundru how the fight went down. Wow, Aundru says. Darn right I said. The bell rings. Alright you guys I'm out, hopefully stuff wears off I say. I sigh and head to class. At first of course I was confrontational, but then I thought about it and spoke when I got called to the counselor's office for some odd reason. So yes, me and Camryn we're still even either way, but if I was gonna make a rumor about somebody, I wouldn't make a rumor about myself. After the intense fight and idiotic rumors we haven't talked since, and for awhile it just stayed that way.

Chapter 13

Secrets And Lies

★ ★ ★

It's been months since the incident from summer. Even though something that's not really situational, it still wasn't adding up. First of all, why did Grandma come to Atlanta unexpectedly? She would usually tell us she's coming, but she didn't, which was unusually odd. Second, why would she stop taking her medicine for a whoe month? It doesn't make sense because what was even the reason. And third, who caused this and what had an effect on what happened. So one night,I overheard Mom on the phone. She's talking to Dad. Something about keeping the same energy when Mom always dropped Big Momma off, but didn't do the same for Grandma. I hide behind a wall the entire time and tiptoe downstairs as I stop at the steps at the wall to listen and stay quiet. Sweetie, I've been dealing with this since I was a child. I can't do this no mo. I'm overgrown now Mom says. Dad is way too nonchalant and is silent. Mom says, I told my mom to leave him. But she just keeps letting him take advantage of her. I love my mama, but I just can't do it anymore. She just needs professional help and within herself.

I paused and stopped listening as I sat on the steps. All I could think of was my Step Grand-Dad and Grandma's mental illness: Schizophrenia as I went deep into these topics and put two in two together. Wait a minute, I say suspiciously. I think back to when Mom was talking to myStep Grand-Dad on the phone right after Grandma was taken away by the authorities. She obviously confronted him. I hardly even remember since I tried to move on, but as I thought back, I reminisced back to the secrets being hidden and lies being told. And then I realized that my Step Grand-Dad was behind all this drama all along that took place back in the summer. Sure, Grandma knew better of course when getting on the bus without letting us know. Even if she wasn't innocent and had part of this, she wanted to see us regardless whether she was stable or not. And I also think back to her not taking the medicine for a month or so and Grandma not leaving him. This means she gets taken advantage of and constantly being manipulated by her listening to him, which is what caused her to be off her meds and ended up having an effect on me and Mom when she tried to visit. Oh my God, now this makes common sense. This whole thing explains it all. I tiptoed back upstairs, but Mom heard me. What are you doing, she asked? I just awkwardly said nothing and went to my room. She was tired anyway. I close the door and back to it as anger boils my blood. I finally found out the truth. I knew it was him all along.

Chapter 14

Family Toxic Drama

★ ★ ★

As I give the backstory, it's a lot more than the incident from summer. Growing up or when I was little my Step-Grand Dad Joey was an alcoholic and drug addict. When I was little, mom and I would be at Grandma's house and there were times when we did hang out. We played basketball, attempted to teach me how to ride a bike,and hung out in the backyard from time to time. Even though it was tolerable, it didn't excuse the dysfunction. The majority of time he would usually be out drinking, smoking, partying, getting drunk and high, basically just getting messed up with all his lil friends or homies. Sometimes I would wait for him to come back, and he wouldn't be back for the whole night.

As I got a little older (11 going on 12) was when I found out about his D.U.I arrests. We did go for a ride one time, but I kept looking back to make sure cop cars didn't recognize his license plate because his driver's license was suspended, but I was used to the dysfunction. And like I said, he would take advantage of Grandma. It would be him cheating allegedly by just having women in the house which I guess were either strippers, just prostitute models or maybe porn stars or just crackheads or whatever. Who knows? He would call my grandma at 2 am to ask her to mail him some money as I see Grandma walk to the mailbox and put in the envelope which had money in it. And this was only so Joey could spend it on drugs and alcohol and overall, just domestic violence or abuse when me and Mom were not around. Where it wouldn't really be physical abuse, but verbal and more emotional abuse. Not only Joey being manipulative to Grandma, but how Grandma would constantly vent about what Joey did to her time and time again but still won't leave him or file for a divorce and would take him back, forgive him. She didn't really have tough skin, but even if she stood up for herself, she still gave him chance after chance every single time. That was the only part that just was frustratingly upsetting to me.

I've never seen my real maternal grandfather. All I knew about him was that he and my grandma did it unprotected. And he was a teen parent and left my grandma after she had my mom at the very young age of sixteen. Nothing was sweet. I did see pictures of my real granddad and sometimes wished that I got to meet him one day.

When Joey was behind all of this from summer it was the last straw, but I wasn't even in shock. I won't say he's evil, but just someone who can be disrespectful by showing fake love and being a jerk at times. It's like he'll stab you in the back.

Chapter 15

An Arch Nemesis
A.K.A My Worst Enemy

———— ★ ★ ★ ————

Meanwhile back in church they were handing out food in the to-go boxes. I got my to-go box, sat in the car and thought it was a barbeque, but it was like fried fish. It seemed suspicious or maybe even dangerous, but a free meal? I had to check it out. Niya comes. Are you eating that? Niya asked shockingly! Yeah, what's wrong with it, I asked? Because Dia cooked it. Once I heard those words, I paused and couldn't believe what I was putting in my mouth. I spit out the food. You can still pray over it, Niya says. Nah, I rather starve than fill my appetite with what she makes, I said as I closed the to-go box.

Meet Dia a.k.a, my aunt on my dad's side of the family. The ratchet, fabulous in the church out of anyone most of all. Somebody who goes around starting stuff, picking fights and beefs with people and always creating her own storms with no one to lend her an umbrella whatsoever. What's also problematic about her is that she's that type of person who never minds her business as her drama track history is extremely high if you go deep within her character. Speaking of her drama track history, it was months ago when she met her match, me and some other people. After service during the offering, she puts the dollar bill in with a nasty attitude. It gets more ratchet from there. I sit at that bench and she comes over with that fake smile and grabs my arm. I swung. I get up as she gets surprised. What's wrong with you, she barks? What's wrong with me? What about you, I point out! Then she says the same line she said to me when I was little. I'm finna go tell yo dad, she quotes! Go on and tell him then, I clapback! It all starts to gather a crowd. Niya stands right next to me. Next thing you know Mom gets involved. I'm his mama, I'm right here, so why can't you tell me? What's the problem she confronts? Dia doesn't say anything to Mom, and just gives her a glare. Everybody just watches and agrees she's messy as hell. Even Niya stood up to her as Dia just fussed at everybody. I grab a bible as I had all my stuff when no one is looking. Ugh, so fake, Niya mumbles. Dia's body language tells Niya to shut up. Dia takes a step towards me. I grunt as I throw the bible in her direction. It almost hits her, but it lands beside her on the bench. C'mon, Niya lets go I say. I leave the church and quickly walk to the car. Niya follows me. You okay, she asked? Yep, I say. Niya tells me about how she said I need help. And so does she, I fire back! Niya never liked Dia, especially when she spread the rumor about Niya that she was cursing and smoking because she unfriended her on Facebook.

Mom comes out of the church. No one talks to me like that, Dia speaks. Touch my son again, mom snaps! And then she heads to the car. They almost got into a fight because mom had enough of her. Dad also talks with me. Probably because Dia was fussing with him about this. All I said to Dad was words like okay, alright, mhmm. Because I knew he was making excuses for her since that's his sister. Yes, let me repeat that's his sister! Which is why she's considered my auntie on his side of the family. I know it's crazy right. After he's done speaking to me, mom and I head home. I told mom that I kicked her car. Now what sense does that make-, mom asks? Mom, would you relax. I'm kidding, I said. She just hugs me and strokes my fro. And that's when Dia became an enemy to everyone else, an arch nemesis on earth.

Chapter 16

Coming Out

--- ★ ★ ★ ---

I felt like it was that time. Whatever they say affects that time, but not for a lifetime. It's like I'm constantly pulling out petals from a flower while saying tell them or tell them not. I told them. Six simple words. I have something to tell you. What is it, mom asks? I am... Asexual. She didn't care. Same with Dad. Fast forward a month later we were at Ihop. Dad mentions this. He also mocks my voice. I don't even talk like that and that's the worst impression by the way. It's nothing, I have just been that way, I said. Mhmm Mom says. We kept talking until the waiter finally arrived with breakfast: Buttery syrup pancakes, ketchup on hash browns and bacon on the same platter together, with a side of orange juice to drink. You know how when you're all conversing and then once the meal arrives, you're just eating and forget about what you were talking about. Yep, that's basically how it went after that. Coming out is not always easy when it comes to what you think. The Good news is that we were all nonchalant about it.

Chapter 17

Curse Mageddon

★ ★ ★

Bad news?

Mom and Dad had a big fight again, and it went a lot more intense than I expected. I was upstairs as I heard a loud bang that made me jump. SWEETIE, WHAT'S WRONG WITH YOU! IS YOU CRAZY, dad snapped! I told you to leave me alone nah, mom quietly snapped! Dad leaves the house startled, acting like he saw Mom with a knife. I run downstairs, and all I see on the ground is a piece of paper along with ice. What, I ask, confused? Mom explains Dad was asking her to pay a bill as usual, but it was at the wrong time when Mom was dealing with an injury. She threw a piece of paper at him and I guess the ice came from his drink as ice fell on the floor when he jumped which I found kind of pathetic since he was going woah, over a piece of paper being thrown at him! But I brushed it off.

As the morning goes by, I talk with Niya on the phone. So, how are you and Terry, y'all doing alright, I ask? Nah, he's been lying, not wanting to get a job and just complaining, she explained. I figured, I predicted. The whole conversation just turns into awkward small talk.

So... the weather I ask? What about it, Niya asks? Never mind, I said. We tell each other bye and end the call.

Next thing you know Mom calls me, JOSEPH she shouts! I ran upstairs. I walk in the restroom and see the jewelry all over the floor. The floor was wet and the bathtub was overflowing. What just happened, I ask? I forgot to turn off the water, Mom says. She also explains that when she realized she forgot to turn off the water, she ran upstairs, slipped and fell while trying to hold on to the jewelry box twisting her leg. She also had buckets in the living room. Oh no I said. Mom runs downstairs. OH Jesus!!! she calls. And that's when a miracle happened. The water finally stops. So does the curse at that moment. We get a ladder and some paint to paint on the ceiling. Mom wonders if Dad was gonna notice. All I knew was that when Dad walks in the house the first thing he notices is furniture. Surprisingly, he didn't care, when Mom told him. I didn't know what was going on and why bad things kept happening a lot lately, but if I was gonna get through this fate, I had to be ready with free will of my own destiny. Especially with something like this.

Chapter 18

Frenemies

———————— ★ ⭐ ★ ————————

I needed a break from this drama.

Fourth period came and Camryn appeared. Yeah, out of all people. We look at each other but don't say anyth ng. You again? Whatever, just what the hell ever I say in my mind. I take a seat. Not that I expected to see Camryn or even deal with him. But if this so-called beef is not gonna be squashed, then we hac to talk it out somehow. But I wasn't bothered since he was nonexistent to me after a while. The teacher gives us time to talk outside the classroom. Okay, look, for once we need to settle this I start off. He agreed to settle it too. It goes deep into Camryn's character to the point where he mentions he has an emotional disorder. Wait a minute. We had our shady moments wher being friends but, you mean to tell me this whole time you were rude to me, took your anger, mean frustration out on me and other people because you have an emotional disorder, I figure out. Yes, he admits. Like I said, insecurities. Even problems from his household where his emotional disorder came from. Just consider this a teachable moment you know. Maybe this is the lesson where you learn that maybe if you didn't project your emotions out on people then bad things wouldn't happen to you, I said.

We kind of wondered why we were being so nice to each other, but yet again we're still starting to get along. We even talked about some of the good times we had when we used to be just friends. I guess we just grew apart and things just started to change I said as he nodded. I mean, I guess we can be friends again he says. Let me think about that for a second, I said. I thought about it. Alright, I made my decision. Well, that was fast Camryn says. Acquainted frenemies I stated. Oh, okay he agreed. This is the first time we ever spoke to each other since our flashback fight. We shook hands and went back to the classroom.

Those times he apologized and the sympathy he gave for the case was nice, but sometimes it was like he was sorry for how I felt or how I reacted not for what he said or his own actions. Sure, a little part of me would've wanted to keep Camryn as a friend, but I don't have to wait around for him to completely change because I know that deep down this still makes him bitter, but a positive person at the same time. Someone who I can throw shade, roll my eyes and consider him a hater, but tolerate and is just okay, even when I deleted his phone number. Some of the stuff he did that was wrong he might see or might not ever see. And you know what that's fine because like I said he is a hater, but a positive person at the same time. We can look back at this and laugh. Because at the end of the day our company doesn't have to be the same as it used to be. I can let go by not caring and wish him nothing but the best as he thinks the same way. Besides something like this which was just not that big of a deal to me. The other bigger problem was something I couldn't be like whatever or roll my eyes after the fact. It went from a typical week to something sinisterly unusual.

Chapter 19

Jinxed

★ ★ ★

Just another regular boring day at school.

Students taking a test, crowded hallways and how the education system is all messed up most of the time. Then we had a fire drill, but it wasn't just any ordinary fire drill. I was just in class and the alarm just rang. I quickly grab my bag. Everybody evacuate the building now, the teacher loudly says! We all quickly walked out of the school building. One kid even shouted FIRE! as a joke! I run to my bus while everyone seems like they're confusingly running for their lives.

The next day everyone is talking about it. Predicted it was either smoke detectors or an actual fire, but most of all a false alarm and that some idiot pulled it. Meanwhile, administrators are on the lookout to find out who did it. I can't believe this happened, Aundru said. Dude I know. Who could've done it? I don't know what to say. That was just weird, Sith says as he goes on his phone. The bell rings. Welp, see you tomorrow I say as I go to my class.

Even at school things got so jinxed just like at home. It was crazy, but a curse that seemed sinister.

Chapter 20

Inside The Warehouse

★ ★ ★

Me and Mom are late for church because of being stuck in traffic due to a car wreck. Out of nowhere Dad calls. The curse strike once again. She breaks the news to me. Somebody robbed and broke into the warehouse at the church. Breaking into the church with just no respect, Mom rants. Wait what, I say to myself! Later on, when putting the money in the basket in the office, I noticed that the back door was open which is the entrance to the warehouse and another way to an exit. I slowly walk to the door. I peeked through the room. It was so dark. All of a sudden, I hear, what are you doing? I put my hands up. I DIDN'T DO IT! I turned around and it was just Niya. Oh, it's just you I say. You sneaking into those snacks in the fridge again, she asked. I mean they do have good snacks but still no. I'm gonna go check the warehouse, I explained. She gets confused as I tell her what happened. Oh lord, Niya says. I know the warehouse is usually locked down but it got broken into. THAT, seems a little suspicious to me, I point out. That's just crazy, Niya says. Well, I'm going in there I say. Are you sure, Niya asks? Dad literally had the keys to lock up the church so it's sealed up during the night, right? Doors and windows closed so these thugs who broke in and stole this stuff obviously came through the gate that is usually open and climbed through the fence. So basically that's how they got in by getting through the back door as another exit which is our way out, I explained. Dang, I sound just like Mom. I don't know- Niya you're coming with me or not, I asked? I take my first step. Wait, I'm going with you, Niya admits! I figured she said that as she said she was not gonna let me go by myself. Alright then let's do this, I said. We both walked in together as the door creaked and closed behind us. We silently walked. We use our cellphones as flashlights like we're using candles. It was so dark and looked abandoned. Flies in the kitchen, the fridge where I got snacks from and random stuff that were in boxes. This feels like a ghost town in here, Niya comments. I know, it always has been. I come in here from time to time, I said. We made it to the exit door as it has a hole where you can peek outside the door and just open it a little bit. There it is the warehouse I said. The door was still open. Oh lord, Niya says! I know, even though it's gonna get situated it still looks empty inside.

Some people who have been in these churches are legendary because of what they're known for. My dad, a preacher, but not as close as Gilbert Patterson or Bishop T.D Jakes and their church looks like an award show on tv. Mom, known as the first lady and was a singer in the choir group before she quit because of how messy it was. And you Niya? Well, you just sit on the bench next to me along with your sister and her kids. As for me I'm just a person who collects offerings by holding a basket that people put money in and return it to the office. As for everyone else either testimonies, first Sundays or either way you're known for something. Wow, Niya comments. I know how deep of a legacy they would have. What do you think ours would be, I ask Niya? She just shrugs. If we survive here without anything bad happening to us, I think we might be the most legendary of all.

Arf! Arf! Arf! We turn and hear dogs barking. They either saw us or heard a loud step to the door as we got shook and walked fast. It's like after investigating we run for our lives like it's a horror movie. Oh, wait in real life it actually was. I almost trip. My hands touch the wooden floor to break my fall. I got back up. I try to find Niya, but it's like she disappeared out of nowhere in the distance. I call her name and look around. I held on to the pole because I almost lost my balance. Woah, I said! From boxes, chairs, open space, even the kitchen as I turned on the light, I didn't see her. Then I see the door and knob banging. I backed away breathing hard. I turned to the other exit, but of course I wasn't trying to risk getting bit by vicious dogs and I didn't know who it was banging on the door with the doorknob rattling so I felt stuck. Stranded and trapped I looked around for something to protect myself, but all I could do was hide behind the wall where the kitchen is as I squinted my eyes and tried to be silent. But then the voice sounded familiar at the door. Then the door barges open with footsteps. I turn to my left and Niya appears. Come on, Niya says. Kay, I whisper. I grab Niya's hand as we rush out and close the door, following by locking it. I was wondering where you were. You left me, I explained. Well because 1, it's time to go and 2, Ma is calling you. C, MON CHILD! Oh, well you would still come back for me regardless, right, I ask? Of course, why wouldn't I, Niya says. It would've just been cruelly selfish, I said. Niya says she does the same as she just smiles. I was getting away from- then I realized the vicious dogs are usually in a fence as they're locked up to begin with. I thought they were free, but the barking was coming from the fence. I guess they are either guard dogs or a new security system for the warehouse. I realized that too, Niya says. The lights turned off as we left when the church was closing for the day.

So far it was mysterious as to why bad things kept on happening and why a lot had gotten worse. I knew I had to get to the bottom of this.

Chapter 21

The Phone Call

---- ★ ★ ★ ----

Can I use your phone, I asked? Why, mom asked? To call Grandma, I lied. For what, she asked suspiciously? To check up on her, I lied again. She gives me the phone anyway. I ran to the restroom and locked the door. Instead of calling Grandma, I called Joey. It was that time, I knew I had to blame him for what he did. The phone is still ringing as I wait for Joey to pick up. He answers, Hello? Hey Joey a.k.a what you put me and some of my family through for years of my life. Uhmm, also how you treat Grandma, I said. What, he asked confusingly? I went on and on about how I felt. The money in the mail that was sent for drugs/alcohol, random chicks and probably dudes from a party he hung out with in the house. Just verbal abuse and everything. He starts playing dumb by saying, I don't know what you're talking about. You don't know what I'm talking about. Okay, F you and I hung up. I left the bathroom. Mom heard me as she obviously wanted to know what happened. I told the conversation word for word. I even censored myself as saying the F word. She was shocked! I gave her back the phone. She calls Joey and explains. I stay furiously silent. I noticed a picture of him that had me in it. I was disgusted as I saw him holding me when I was a baby.

I ran upstairs in rage, grabbed a plastic bat and slammed it on the picture. I HATE YOU! I repeat. Mom grabs and hugs me on the couch while I was punching the table. Mom asked, Why do you hate him so bad? Because of what he did I said, as that's all I can say. She just hugs me as I dry my eyes and my facial expression looks like I'm just over it.

Days later it's after church. What's wrong, Niya convincingly asked? Nothing, nothing happened okay. No, what's wrong, Niya, convincingly asked again? Fine, I'll tell you, So I gave in and told her everything. YOU CUSSED HIM OUT, Niya exclaims shockingly! Well yeah, but it wasn't like that. It was just, I said what I wanted to say and hung up. Wow, Niya says. She gets distracted about vacation. NIYA, I snapped! Sorry, it's just bad enough that I had a fight with my Step Grandad. I just don't have time to be thinking about vacation right now. You want to make me feel better. Tell me the time where somebody did you wrong. Niya tells me about her sister, birth mom and most of her family in general and why they do her wrong a lot.

I could've said leave me alone,but I just related to her as she told me to hang in there. I was upset throughout the whole weekend, but just over it as I held Joey accountable for having resentment. He also didn't expect it when I poured the cup of telling him how it is when saying you're a manipulative, narcissistic, sociopath as everybody in the family knows. I still love him because family is family no matter what, but by a distance. Sometimes it's hard to love somebody when they have done terrible things to you or to someone else you care about.

Chapter 22

Therapy

After the heated phone call with Joey, Monday comes by and I get checked n for a therapy session. It's not any different than seeing a counselor, but laying on a couch. It looked weird because it looked like an abandoned house as I looked around. Mom and I got checked in and sat in the waiting room until we got called in. The therapist asked us questions of course. The session went on for like an hour. So we talked about things like, Self-harm when coping that obviously stopped, what happened with the phone call between me and Joey and just family drama as a whole. I nod the whole time. Words like I don't know, yeah, nope, I don't remember, never even thought about suicide and so on. It gets personal when it comes to Joey and how he was the mastermind behind the incident last summer as I scolded him on that too. I didn't need to or even wanted to see him. I didn't want to or needed to, I said to the therapist. Mom gets concerned. She also mentions my demeanor and how I don't talk when it comes to issues most of the time. As the session ends when done with her clipboard that she wrote on, she didn't just say "mhmm" throughout the session. When we walked out of the session, I said one more sentence. I'm here because this is something I can't control. I can't control what my step granddad has done, but I can only speak my mind for what he's done. The final question: if I was in my grandma's shoes what would you do or what would you say to him? It would be how I said it to him on the phone but stepping into her shoes like the same energy on that phone call. I said, I'd wished he would've done it to me because there's no way that I would've let him verbally abuse and do that to me too.

After we left therapy, I thought it was over, but of course it wasn't. Once you think it's over it's not over. Next thing you know high stakes start to hit us. Not just Mom losing her wallet at a Barbeque restaurant earlier that night when she had to go back to find it as she kept on praying that it would be there after leaving Walgreens. But somebody hacked into Mom's bank account at 4 A.M in the morning. She got her money back though. Her wallet was found and saved, but not the restaurant. It was just randomly on the ground at the parking lot. That's when I knew the curse moved again. Why was the Barbeque restaurant not saved? As soon as we came back, a fire truck appeared as I guess a fire happened with burning smoke along with an ambulance and police sirens. Firefighters put out the flames with a spraying hose, people were just in shock, and as we drove off mom and I were shocked as well about the restaurant. But Mom thanked the Lord as I just sighed.

Chapter 23

Moment Of Plot
Twist Revealed

--- ★ ★ ★ ---

The plot thickens.

After service at church I was talking with Nett. We talked a lot. Especially his story of wondering if his parents would accept him for being gay or becoming a trans male. Anyway, everybody was talking about Dia once again. Nett tells me the tea. You were right about Dia, she is doing voodoo, he says. At first, I didn't believe it because I thought somebody was just making stuff up either for attention or they just didn't like her or had a problem with her so they spread this allegedly just to be messy and probably for whatever reason. I doubted it at first even though a lot of people said I was right.

What? No way. She can be messy,but that's just crossing the line, I said. Nah, it's true. She made a deal with the devil Nett says. She's been the devil I point out. But then I thought about it. With all the bad things continuing to happen to me, close friends and family, Dia was not just messy but also pure evil. So I figured it would make sense, but I didn't want to jump to conclusions.

Meanwhile, at school when I talked about not just the phone call, but my aunt with Sith that's when I thought of a plan as I explained to Sith. The church wasn't like any other day. Well, not them talking about Dia was unusual but what I found out it wasn't like any other. Sith was obviously shook. To expose her, but wait if I was gonna expose Dia, I had to have the facts. There was only one thing I had to do so I wouldn't jump into conclusions too quick and look or feel dumb. Look up and research voodoo, hexes, witchcraft and e.t.c. I know it's disturbing. And then I think back to the food she sold at the church. Honestly it didn't hurt. It was delicious until you found out it could be poisonous. But yet again I didn't want to jump to conclusions.

Next Sunday I went to the office to talk with Dad and Nett. Nett knows more information and so does Dad, well because that's his sister. I had all the receipts ready. Nett, what happened, I asked? What happened? Well, all I know is in her soul, her spirit is crazy but other than that I don't know what else to tell you, he explains. This whole plot twist was straight dead on. Dad understood the factual evidence from what I wrote and it was especially easy when people know the type of person she is. Also information from Dad since he knows about his sister and sugarcoats it as the plan worked and she finally wasn't there to notice the moment of truth. Nett, thank you, I say. I leave the office. I looked around sure enough she wasn't there, but Niya was as I told her everything. I know you texted me last night but wow, she says! She tells me about when she ate Dia's food and it made her sick. Well, are you alright? What did she do to you, I asked? I think it was food poisoning, she explains. She's not gonna get away with this, I said. She is crazy, Niya says. More like a monster I say as she agrees. Church closes. Bye, later I say. Buh bye, later gator, Niya says. I look at her like really but give a snicker.

On a serious note there was only one problem. Dia may be evil, but she ain't stupid. After I talked to Dad and Nett about it in the office it got everybody talking. Even while preaching, Dad mentioned it one time. Instead of hot gospel it was hot gossip. Everything was he said- she said drama. Dia never stayed in her lane as usual. She talked with her brother, (Dad) about what is being talked about around church. How do I know about this? Because 1, it's predictable, 2, she would usually do something like this and 3, she's with Dad the most because he tolerates her. The reason why she does witchcraft? For obvious reasons to put hexes on people especially for people she doesn't like including Niya, definitely Mom, maybe my close friends, others and now me as I'm one of them. The cursed victims. She gets revenge by wishing worse on others even for no reason. Magic can be good or bad but it was bad. It was evil voodoo in cold blood as it happens. But Dia I knew she was no good: Bleached blonde box braids didn't see it coming I said to Niya earlier. It should've ended after Dia was exposed, but one thing led to another. The toxic warzone continued as Dia was the breaking news and talk of the church. God may not like ugly, but it was showing. Along with jealousy of what people have, that they don't have, thinking you were cool with so and so. But hey people change, going through mentally thinking drugs and alcohol will ease the pain.

It gets more loco when a fight breaks out in the church from sister Felicia and someone else from what I overheard from Dad. I knew it was Dia's dangerous evil plot. But it's gonna take more than poisonous barbecue food and spiritual witchcraft to do me, my people and others in. It hurts to see the people you love be affected by evil doesn't it? Well, it does. Unexpectedly, I looked like the correct one. Cause I played the part of having people saying I should've listened to you. That I was right about her. I was glad more people knew she was not a good person. Just like how I exactly wanted more to realize but even I didn't realize that she would be more hated for something like this than just bringing out a ball of negative energy and negativity by being toxic. Everyone was shocked and disturbed about why she was talked about, even though she made me uncomfortable as well. Some people say she just sold her soul or made a deal with the devil. But I think what people meant was that how I and they realized that it was more to her character than being a full actual grown older woman who is just a ghetto hoodrat that is delusional and problematic. She was a pure evil soul that wanted to project evil to people due to vengeance, jealousy of success and people she had beef with without us knowing the details about her. If she can cause toxic storms and warzones by picking fights, run people off and passes around the toxic energy by being the you problem and is capable of constantly being an issue to everyone else than she's capable of being a worst enemy or better yet even capable of being a true definition of being an archnemesis to the world.

Chapter 24

One Thriller Weekend

★ ⭐ ★

It was Friday.

The weekend is here. Spring is in the air up in the blue sky. I walk down the hallway as I throw my backpack to the wall because of a rough morning of going through it as I grunt. I had my head down. I looked up and there was Jamie. I realized about an argument we had about mental health as I got offended. Even when I spoke about it with Nio. What happened with you and Jamie, he asked? I mean we're fine, we're just not talking right now so… yeah, I say at the moment as I give a flashback. I apologized to Jamie about it, explained why I got offended because my family deals with it, and also made a point about what if it happened to you also by using an example. Well, it would just make me mad, Jamie says. Jamie sometimes thought I was jealous because he hung out with people I don't like, but at the end of the day it's like why should I care who Jamie hangs out with even Camryn, a frenemy acquaintance who I let my close friends know about. We had some nostalgia together but think we've been cool but just associates all along. Either way I don' need a one-sided friendship, not when I have close friends. The bel rings and we head to class as I try to be excited for the weekend.

Lunch comes and I warn Sith and Aundru about this event where they and I are facing as they're concerned. You guys heard worse, but you've never heard or seen a crisis like this before, I say in a serious tone. I know that already, your aunt has issues, Sith says. I don't even consider her a real aunt; I consider her a villain that's related, I say. So, what are you gonna do, Aundru asked? What I know how to do, speak out, I explained. Not just to go there, use my power against her which was already physical from what you guys already know about me throwing a book at her. But with my voice to diss and throw shade at her verbally, then go sit my behind back down. I mean about not just what she caused, but everything toxic in general. Speaking out may not help but neither is just talking about it. It almost destroyed my friendships with you guys as crazy unexpected stuff happened with us as well. My nemesis threatened me and cursed me along with my family(spiritually), somebody broke into my dad's warehouse and stole stuff. Yeah all of that. I went through this destiny all for what, just so fate can slap me in the face and I wouldn't get a chance to use my free will just because I'm in a position on a curse not being lifted yet and know what I must have to do. I've seen the toxic war in the church by an evil soul of an archnemesis herself who uses voodoo for revenge, her worst enemies she had beef with and just pure evilness. Nobody wants to call it out or speak about it and some will let this slide, just spill gossip tea and toxic shade... that's fine. If no one's gonna speak up, then I will. Sith and Aundru see where I'm coming from as they agreed to help. I have your back, Sith says. It's like she's Satan, Aundru says. Um because she is. I just gotta do what I gotta do, I say. What if, they say. I know you guys want to do something to help, but no I'm sorry. This is something I must do on my own, I said as they understood. I get up from my seat and walk off from the table.

I got home. I went upstairs to my room, plopped my stuff and threw myself to my bed. Body language just screams, punch, hit, kick anything and everything. Just let it out, but again trying to enjoy the weekend. Later that night I was trying to enjoy the perfect time of the night which is the weekend. A complete coincidence to celebrate three in a half days of being dsmissed from school and work. wos no longer feeling pissed off with anger, goosebumps and blood boiling. I didn't have a stomach acne or choked from my snacks. I didn't think of being paranoid by an evil wind with the worst things coming towards me. It was just a count of blessings as I was chilling in my room. It was the calm perfect way to end a Friday night until I woke up with a nosebleed. It was nothing new since I had them before as I used to run to Mom when I was little because... well shoot, I didn't know what to do. Now I just stick a tissue in my nostril. I ran to the restroom. It's so bloody like a bloodbath but it's almost dripping. I get a tissue or find a tampon to stop the blood, as tampons work well to stop nosebleeds. I get dizzy...BAM! I hit my head on the door. My body is thrown to the ground. I blacked out. I woke up. It's morning. I look around. I'm still in the same bathroom. I get up and look at myself in the mirror. Dried up blood was still on my face. It looked like a scar that felt like I backed down from a showdown. It looked like I got jumped on. But the way my expression looked in the mirror I was staring with a determined glare on me looking beat up. I looked around again, no stains of blood anywhere in sight, so I didn't have to clean up. I assumed it was Dia doing her voodoo tricks on us again. So evil and full of hatred to the point where not imma kill you but it's imma injure you. I turn the door knob and kick it to the side. I sprinted to the fridge to go get myself an ice pack for my forehead and I sat on the couch. Then Mom walks in. What happened to your head, she asked? I explained what happened. Do I need to take you to the hospital, she asked? No, I answered.

Saturday morning continues. Dad walks in as he gets ready for work. I sense an argument kick in when he's talking about a bill. I raise my hands up like angels are all over me. Stop, I silently shout! How much do we have to go through to end it all? Enough is enough, I muttered. Dad leaves as usual. Every weekend there's always something, Mom says. She goes to work at home in her office. I go to my log in the backyard where I go to think and calm down. I sit on the log as dirty mud gets on me when I tripped on grass. Even earlier I mentioned to Mom that we're being jinxed when she mentioned Dia. I ain't trying to go to jail, but if she touches me she's gonna get popped. YOU CRAZY WITCH, she snapped!

Later on, it's nighttime. Mom comes back from the store after getting some things. Everything was fine until VROOMSHHH, the car wouldn't start. The engine is not starting I said. I start seeing smoke. I tried pushing the key remote to the car. No luck. I have insurance, Mom clears up. She opens the hood while I go to the store to get help. The lady who worked there recognized me. Joseph, I haven't seen you in so long, she said. Yeah, but right now it's an emergency. Our car broke down and we need to find some help, I said. She didn't know what to do so again no luck. But then a guy comes, and we get a miracle as Mom calls for help. It turns out there was something wrong with the battery. He fixed it, we thanked him and he left. We rushed to the store. We get a coca cola soda and pour it on the rusty engine while lifting up the hood of a car using a flashlight app on my phone. And that was my tomboy skills, Mom brags. She was referring to her younger days. We get in the car and make it home.

It is now Sunday. It's a quiet ride to the church in Glenwood through traffic. With all the stuff going on at church, I had to speak out. We make it to church. I step out of the car. Where are you going, mom asked? I kept walking as determination kicked in. I say hey to the piano guy, Mel. He mentions what he noticed too. I open the door and then I see him, Pastor Johnny. I go up and talk to him. He asks me questions like how's life, school and e.t.c. I get to the point and tell him that I have a testimony. You're sure you're ready to go up there, he asked me. I nod. Alright then, we'll have you up when service is almost over, he says. I thanked him and went back to my seat. More people started to come in as this time it was a huge audience. Niya comes with her wanna be husband Terry and as usual sits right next to me and the routine starts. Choir sings. We take a cracker that tastes like paper and take some grape juice that looks like wine since it was the first Sunday. We ate and drank and lastly Dad preached and everyone said prayer after that. Next thing you know, out of nowhere Dia shows up. Speak of the devil, Niya says. I hate her, I said. Hate is a strong word, Niya says. It's also a feeling of emotions, I said. Me too, she says. She was around the back doing whatever she was doing. She only comes to church when Dad is around. She walks in looking ratchet as hell with her bonnet on. Hey, this isn't me slut shaming, this is me saying she looks ridiculous. I'm not the only one pissed despising her with determination; others were too. It was time for me to go up. I tell Niya to watch my stuff. I'm going up there, I said. Wait a minute whatcha bout to do, Niya whispers? You and everybody else will see, I whispered back. I take off my jacket and step on the pulpit as Pastor Johnny hands me the microphone. It felt like I was holding a sword or a bullhorn. I got up there in front of the crowd to give my testimony and just speak out. But one person can be that bold to make a difference or go deep. I can't change the world or people's minds but I can use my voice as my biggest weapon. I check to see if the mic is on. If it's not a testimony then it was something I had to say. My- I pause. This is my only chance. I couldn't be a coward and back down now. Too late for that! I was put in this position for a reason and I knew I had to do something once and for all. MY NAME IS JOSEPH. AND... I'M THE ONE WHO HAS SOMETHING TO SAY. I HAVE A VOICE! I get so many yeahs and amens. BUT SO DO YALL. WHO WE ARE WE ALL HAVE A VOICE TO A TESTIMONY. PREACH, somebody says in the crowd! It starts to amp and pump me up. TURNING AGAINST EACH OTHER. I turn and side eye to Dia. Her lips are poked out, disgusted with an attitude and rolling her eyes. SNAKES WHO WISH AND DO EVIL TO OTHERS. AND NOT JUST TRAGEDY BUT TOXIC ENERGY. Everyone starts to cheer me on. It took a lot of courage but dang it felt good. They urge me on even more. PEOPLE WANT TO TALK ABOUT WHAT THEY GO THROUGH. BUT IT'S NOT JUST ABOUT WHAT YOU GO THROUGH. IT'S ABOUT WHAT WE PUT EACH OTHER THROUGH. WE PUT EACH OTHER THROUGH IT. WE PUT HATE ON HATE AGAINST EACH OTHER, I yelled out! Take your time Pastor Johnny says. Then a quote popped into my head. I don't need your drama because I believe in karma. I repeated again. I encourage people to say it. When I don't need your irrelevant drama, you say because I believe in instant karma. I DON'T NEED YOUR- IRRELEVANT DRAMA! BECAUSE I BELIEVE IN- INSTANT KARMA! AGAIN! As we chant. Gotta stay strong. I DON'T NEED YOUR- IRRELEVANT DRAMA!! BECAUSE I BELIEVE IN- INSTANT KARMA!! I don't need it! Say it like you mean it! ONE MORE TIME! I DON'T NEED YOUR- IRRELEVANT DRAMA!!! BECAUSE I BELIEVE IN- INSTANT KARMA!!!. I DON'T NEED IT. DON'T NEED IT! YOU HEAR ME? EXACTLY, I DON'T NEED IT. I had my hand raised. Everyone starts to clap and folks start praising. Even somebody almost cried due to feeling the hurt in my voice. I give the mic back to Pastor Johnny, jump off the pulpit and walk to where the door was. I was breathing hard. Nett hugs me. Not bad at all Joe.T, not bad at all. You better speak the truth, he says. I stood next to Niya. You okay, she asked disturbingly? Yeah, I'm good, I answered. Dad finishes with a prayer and service is over. Everybody leaves as I get hugs, handshakes and compliments. This whole thing got Sister Felecia and Nett talking. Some though that in the future I would be a preacher or something in activism. I never thought of that, but I took it as a compliment. I looked outside and it was raining and thunderstorming just like how we went through this storm. I sit on the bench to calm down. Hey, I turned and there's Niya. She's wearing a blue hoodie with glasses as she used to have dreadlocks, but she cut it and now her hair is short. I saw you up there. That was so brave. I thought you were about to cry. I couldn't even get up there and do that, but dang you took it kind of far, she says. Yeah, I kinda did, I said. That was some real deep stuff Niya said. H.O.M.I.E.W.A.R.R.I.O.R.S. this was it. I don't need your irrelevant drama because I believe in instant karma.

Look at Dia. She's the villain of the drama. She may have won the battle by getting revenge but she lost the war. The result of a destiny. The Homies stayed thick and thin as the warriors stayed strong through it. She puts curses on people, but it's like she cursed herself being satanic when the tables turned on her by getting fired from Dad's businesses. Someone roasted her that she's adopted since she's entitled about Dad being her real "brother". Even Dad said that she not only has drug problems, but problems with herself as karma continues to go hard and mess her up physically, mentally and emotionally. All because of being the evil antagonist to not just me a protagonist but a nemesis to everybody. It's not just about what you go through. It's about what we put each other through. But we can break this wash, rinse, and repeat a cycle, I say as I try to be ceep.

Me and Niya tried to be serious but we couldn't help it and we just started cracking up. Even when I told Niya that shade was thrown by Dia and she snickers.

So, where's Terry, I asked? He's out in the car, waiting for me which I'm not even gonna bother being rushed by him, she says as she starts ranting about him. By not liking church and only caring about eating snacks, sleeping, not going to work and expecting her to always cook and clean while he plays fortnite all day. Plus him being cocky and arrogant along with his crappy attitude which by the way was the reason why Niya came to church late and sat next to me while being annoyed because she wanted to come early. But due to Terry, she was late.

Well, there goes the church. This is our final time coming here. Are you gonna miss it, I asked Niya? Without you and Ma here, yeah. You did it she says. No, Niya we did it together, I corrected. Lights go out and it was time to go. The weather is no joke as it kept raining hard. Dia is just sitting there at her stand, selling nasty barbeque food that makes people sick or have food poisoning. Some came but left. Fine, whatever, I ain't got time for this anyway, she mumbles. I sucked my teeth followed by Niya and I not caring. Nobody wanted to fool with her as she looked like she's over it. Me and Mom got in the car as a guy who we call Cowman was working on our car. The battery was good as new but it smelled like weed. I knew because Cowman was smoking marijuana from what they have in the back outside of the church as his eyes were bloodshot red. Me and Mom say bye to Niya. Terry honks the horn. Come on, he yells! I'm coming, shoot, Niya yells back! Stay strong I say to her. You know I will, she says.

Even people like Josh, my half-brother, mentioned what I did and a woman named Carmine who Mom is jealous of, since she flirts with Dad gave support as well. I guess I can say I'm legendary for not just collecting the tithes and offering in church, but someone that took the initiative for what no one in this church had ever done before.

Which was controversial, but spoke volumes about a toxic environmental war zone where we should be praising God and helping others in (the church). Basically nobody ever had the boldness and bravery to call it out before.

We made it back home. I put my van shoes away. Mom wishes she was more confident like me when she was younger. She walks in and hugs me. I'm really proud of you, she says as we go downstairs for dinner. The curse was officially lifted. I gotta say this has been one messed up weekend. A thriller. But you know what, even if this adventure couldn't make it better not for just me, but for me and my people. We went through it together. That's what mattered.

Chapter 25

The Visit

— ★ ★ ★ —

It's now a year later and everybody has gone their separate ways. Niya moves away to Indiana to get away from Terry, her ex-husband for him being a jerk, having a disease and for cheating, as she looked on his phone and found a dating app on it, which counts as cheating. It was sad to see her move but I know that she had to do it for her own good and now she is happily living single. Dad still preaches at the church, but mom and I don't go there every Sunday anymore. I mean when I got older, we didn't go every Sunday at times. But now it's not as much. Most of the time we only go there for a special Holiday or occasion. God finally answered her prayers since she said the church is just too toxic.

At school I told Sith and Aundru what happened and what went down. Aundru thinks I'm so dope. Sith starts ranting about his sister Paidon but what I did, he thought was so worth it. And trust me, it was. Tuh, bye to the witch I said. And after that we had the last laugh. Nobody wanted to be associated with Dia ever since she got fired from Dad's businesses along with her toxicity as she tried to frame and wish evil on the businesses. The employees and manager a.k.a boss didn't want to be bothered by her, possibly by people who don't know her. Even Dad knew she had problems within herself. Her storms no longer applied. And as for everyone else they moved on and not that many people go to the church as Sister Felicia and Dad would be there from time to time but they moved to a different church in another area. He still preaches at the church on Glenwood, but not as much. As for me, I'm still hanging in there. Back on the grind as usual. Being away from the church I grew up at won't be the same when it's preached anywhere else for sure, but yet again neither will everything else in the church. It wasn't too toxic after a while but it wasn't peaceful either, since everybody and I cleaned out their stuff. For one thing, I won't say it's dead but it's just buried alive. On that note It's just meant to be that way. Other than that, at this or that point everything is back to normal, and it was all good again until it was one more thing I realized and had to do. I found out that we were going to visit my grandparent's house. Oh God. Basically, we were going to see them or is it the other way around. Whatever it was, I knew I couldn't go through this again, but I also knew that if I was gonna try to completely rebuild to be rebuilt for this bond with Grandma, I had to visit her, see uncle June and deal with Joey because that phone call was the last time we ever talked.

It was a 6 or 7 hour drive from going all the way from Atlanta, Georgia to Memphis, Tennessee. Even longer when we pulled over for restroom stops and got lunch from Wendy's. We head back on the road. We make it to Memphis and head to Grandma's house as we park in her driveway. Mom goes to say hey to her brother, her mom and Step-Dad. I get the suitcases out of the trunk and walk into the house. I stop at the front door. Well, here goes nothing, I say to myself. I was about to knock on the door or was about to ring the doorbell, but the door was open. I sighed and opened the screen door. There I was, in the house. The first person I saw was Joey. Aye Boy, Joey says! I guess he forgot about the phone call. Hey...you...I hesitate. He goes outside to get the rest of our stuff from the trunk. I say hey to June, Mom's brother. He doesn't really talk much. Well at least not to me. Then I see Grandma. She still had the perm along with her gold tooth. Hey I said as we hugged. Hey, she says back. Joey is done getting the bags as Mom and I head upstairs to the guest room. We walk in and unpack. I noticed a hole in the wall. It looked molded like a dam. I asked Grandma, uh what is with the hole in the wall. Oh, there's a leak and when it rains it will soak through the house. Joey said he was gonna call somebody to fix it, but he didn't, she explained. Oh, I say. Then small talk comes in. So...how are you doing? I awkwardly start the conversation. Fine she says. Mom comes in. Her and Grandma talked for a little bit and she left the room. It was so hot because the air conditioning was not working, so we had to use a fan the entire time of the visit. I looked around and reminisced about the house. The same kitchen where Joey is a barber and does hair. The couch that had a mattress inside and the townhouse at the hood which is Mom's childhood home. There were no locks on the door, so I had to use the old chair blocking the door trick. The trip was only for three days but to Mom it felt like all of eternity or in this case forever.

The whole weekend was just random. June walked into our guest room at about 3 am in the morning to write something on paper, ball it up and throw it in the trash which got Mom fussing and irritated I was about to go to sleep. We went shopping with Grandma and she almost made a scene due to her mental illness at the store.

Following that she was arguing with Joey by genuinely standing up finally for herself for once in front of company and me seeing Joey drunk for the first time. Even when Mom's best friend Stefani and her kids Saria and Gracia were there, he was walking funny, trying to get attention by making a fool out of himself and throwing up. He wasn't even sober. Just an obnoxious drunk who couldn't hold his beer, wine, liquor, whisky, champagne or whatever alcoholic beverage he used in bottles or shot glasses. His dialogue was kind of funny though. Do you know what life is? Do you know what a game is? He even gets spiritual when he says I'M GOING STRAIGHT TO HELL- I MEAN HEAVEN! Everybody laughed at that line. Heck, he even made me crackup. I may have despised his actions, but he sure is entertaining. Even when he is drunk as hell by dialogue. Company leaves as he laid down on the couch to sleep it off. I turned off the lights. It looked like Joey was talking but mumbling in his dream. Since he went nite-nite, I threw a blanket on him and went upstairs to the guest room. Grandma says that Joey will be turning up for his birthday. Nah man. You fall out, throw up puke, barf, vomit by drinking too much and all this stuff. You are too old for that mom rants. That's what he said, says Grandma. She wanted to know where he was. He's downstairs, I said. He's just knocked out cold asleep I explained. Grandma leaves as June, mom and I go to sleep.

Last night there were fireworks. Obviously because we visited around the 4th of July. After eating a barbeque around midright there were no fireworks, but firecracker sounds. Turns out it wasn't firecrackers. It was gunshots!! POW! One gunshot. POW! POW! Two gunshots. POW! POW! POW! Three gunshots. I duck my head like it's New Year's. It stopped around 1:00 am. I couldn't sleep but I finally dozed off.

It's Monday morning as me and Mom made it and survived three days of family dysfunction. Mom was definitely ready to go home. I told her it wasn't too bad. She was just relieved. I look at the picture of our family reunion. Uncles, aunts, cousins, my great grandmother who died before I was born or existed and grandfather, basically before I was alive in the world. My aunt Julie who's easy to manipulate because when she is fussing, I tell her she is pretty, and she stops because of the compliment. My cousin Jayden, we're not close, but still close enough. He's someone who has ADHD, but makes me laugh because of the stuff he does. Also, he's somebody who got expelled from every school in Memphis and can be a bad influence, but is fun to hang around. There's cousin C who is not on good terms with Jayden but it's cool. And lastly, cousin Deke who's loyal and close to Mom.

It's breakfast time as Mom and I ate while June watched girls twerking on YouTube on the tv. Of course it gets awkward so he turns the tv off. Joey walks into the kitchen. He's finally awake from last night. You had a wild night I comment. Wait what, says Joey. He barely remembered anything that happened last night when he was intoxicated. Never mind, I said and I went back to eating my cereal. After the grocery store, Mom and I started to pack up and check to see if we had everything so it wouldn't be lost. Joey helped to load our stuff in the trunk as I double checked to see if we had everything.

Grandma comes in, Stacy telling you to come on, she says. I know, I'm just checking, I said. You remember what happened when I told you when you were helping me work my phone, she asked. Uh yeah what about it? When I came down to Georgia and yall told me I wasn't well and then I made yall upset. I stopped packing for a second when she mentioned the regrets of the mistake she made. Oh, that. Well, I got over it a week later so yes it was...upsetting but I knew I had to move on. We can outweigh this, I explained. Grandma even mentioned calling Mom about Joey many times. She sighs. I guess I still feel bad to this day even though it was years ago, she says. Well, it's not too late to let go, I said as I smiled. She smiles back as we hug each other. We walk downstairs to the car together as we talk about nostalgic memories from when she visited before the incident happened.

Even if I never forget this experience, at the end of the day it was just a dysfunctional weekend. But me and everybody else including Grandma became somewhat, good now, closer now and rebuilt an unconditional relationship as we might as well just be happy. I carry my bag anc get in the car as we all tell each other bye. Mom and I drove off, stopped by a barbeque restaurant and left Memphis, Tennessee to co back home to Georgia. We visited. We experienced it. We rebuilt.

Chapter 26

Bring It On

★ ★ ★

EPILOGUE:Finale

Once upon a time there was a homie warrior named Joseph a.k.a, Joe.T.

A person who's down to earth but a savage. A character who is stronger than weak, independent and is never afraid to stand up for himself. And just somebody who tries to have opportunities that finds success which comes with side hustles and negative controversial shenanigans of antics, but can turn to a positive hustle at what he does. Someone who is blunt about his dysfunctional home life, but didn't mention it too much because he didn't want people to feel bad for him or at least not because of people anymore. TMI, sure but why should I avoid my issues by not talking about it just because it would look like it's all about getting sympathy. This whole thing wasn't just memorable moments of something situational that is like an episode. These were scenes of chapters of what I and some of my people went through. And for young adulthood or for the rest of my life, I will always remember how this event went down as I wrote in a diary or journal narrating this. I even found out that HomieWarrior meant something else as well, Survivor. Is this like a fairytale? No. But this could be happily ever after. This may be dark, twisted and messed up, but I didn't get this far just to not have a happy ending.

I will let go. But I'll never forget. I'm not embarrassingly ashamed, I don't feel bad and I don't regret how this happened because it just happened. I get you might feel bad, but you don't have to feel sorry for me. Why? Because I'm unapologetic for the way I am. For something that's so intense like a lifetime movie; I don't always need to tell my life story just for an excuse on why I'm like this. I'm a savage for a reason. I can't change that. If you're close to me, and if you know where I came from or what I have been or went through then you would know. But the role I play in this world of society doesn't always see that, and that's okay. In some moments, I may not be proud of my personality getting aggressively destroyed, but I'm not sorry for my character. I'm not sorry for not being convinced that it was something I had to be and I'm not sorry that you don't know me.

Even though you read this "movie" event, I think you somewhat know me. But I'm still unapologetic. It would've been easy to just give up. If it was only about grandma: a family member fighting her demons, schizophrenia, what happened that summer, the vacation, an arch nemesis causing a toxic warzone, fake friends who are not really your friends to begin with and just all of the above. But it was more than that. I guess if I learned anything throughout all of this you could say that somebody out there has it worse than you. But when it comes to having issues like a human being and I mean real issues in yourself the best thing is to just be strong. I still spiritually believe in curses though. But sometimes there's no explanation on why bad things or good things can happen to a person. You either deal with it or let it break you. You either become an evil monster or a strong person. You either make life harder as life's short but shorter for yourself than living your life or move on from irrelevant fuckery. Your choice.

When we stopped by at the Barbeque restaurant the visualization from this event as I thought about it was like the hero or HomieWarrior. Fighting for my close people against the nemesis till the end. Using my defensive power basically and that's what it was from the start and how it is in the end and had to be in the darkness before I can be into the light. After thinking about it, Mom and I were on the road laughing, smiling and talking about the trip as we drove home.

Truth is... I can't say this is the end overall. After all of this me and my closest friends and mostly family aren't so different as we are finally ready to let each other grow up from irrelevant toxicity that got us through something that was destined in a way. And no matter what happens we will always be there for each other.

BRING IT ON!

The End